A Pig Called Henry

Tudor stories linking in with the
National Curriculum Key Stage 2

First published in 1995 by Watts Books
96 Leonard Street, London EC2A 4RH

Franklin Watts Australia
14 Mars Road
Lane Cove
NSW 2006

Series editor: Paula Borton
Consultant: Joan Blyth
Designer: Nina Kingsbury

A CIP catalogue record for this book
is available from the British Library.

ISBN 0 7496 2204 0

Dewey Classification 942.05

Printed in Great Britain

A Pig Called Henry

by
Karen Wallace

Illustrations by Martin Remphry

Watts Books
London ● New York ● Sydney

To Edge

1

Arthur Goes Shopping

Arthur Knucklebone sat on an oak stump in the dark, smelly kitchen of his mother's cottage and dunked last week's bread into a bowl of runny porridge. It tasted disgusting.

He kicked the earth floor with a ragged

shoe. Arthur Knucklebone was in a bad
mood. Today was market day in the
village and his mother had told him to sell
his pet pig, Henry. What's more, she had
forced him to wear his itchy brown
breeches and his even itchier woollen shirt.
"You won't get a penny for that pig if you
look like one yourself," she had bellowed

at him early that morning.

Arthur wiped his mouth on his sleeve
and stared gloomily around him. The
room was dark because hardly any light
came through the greased linen tacked
over the window and it was smelly because
of the iron pot full of murky green liquid
that bubbled slowly over the fire.

Arthur wrinkled his nose. There was always something nasty bubbling in that pot. It was either his supper or one of his mother's potions. Because Old Mother Knucklebone was in the business of cures. She made up disgusting ointments and vile potions to make sick people better. Her most popular one was bubbling now, a mixture of dandelion leaves, rotten onions and chopped frogs.

By the time the liquid had boiled down to a kind of gluey paste, it was certain to cure all coughs, colds, aches and pains. And since everyone they knew lived in damp, smelly cottages and ate last

week's bread and porridge, Old Mother
Knucklebone did quite well.

Arthur looked up as the front door
swung open and his mother stomped into
the room. Her beaky face was purple with
rage. "That pig of yours has just rolled in
my cabbages," she yelled. "How can I
make my baldness cure from *crushed*
cabbages?" She glared at him. "You know
perfectly well they have to be wrapped
whole in a fox's skin and buried for a

week."

Arthur carried on chewing. He didn't
believe in any of his mother's medicines,
ever since she told him to rub pigeon dung
on his cuts to make them better. He
winced at the memory of how the cuts
went poisonous. "You must have used
chicken droppings by mistake," was all his
mother could say.

"There's two thieves to be branded at

market today," said Arthur, hoping to take his mother's mind off her cabbages. "Jack Jones, next door, says so."

Ma Knucklebone cocked her head. There was nothing she liked better than a good branding. Except, that is, for a good hanging, especially on a sunny day like this one.

"I'd come to market with you," she said sadly. "But it's fine drying weather and almost a year since the linen's been wetted."

Arthur shrugged. He never knew why his mother was so fussy about washing things. They only got dirty again.

Old Mother Knucklebone held out a penny in her grimy hand. "Six herrings, twenty candles - best tallow mind, a block of salt and some more of that nice brown woollen cloth."

Arthur wriggled in his shirt. "But it's rough and itchy," he complained. "Besides, how will I know where to find it?"

His mother rolled her eyes. "Look for the signs above the shops," she said. "You went to school, didn't you?"

Arthur sighed. Across the room the wooden slate he had used in school hung on the wall. He never did learn to read that strange long word that began with A and ended with Z. In fact all Arthur could remember about the school was the master's cane whacking his head or his hands or the back of his neck. And it

wasn't just him. All the other boys got the same treatment.

"You don't have to *read* the signs," explained his mother. "Lots of people can't read. There's pictures to tell you. And once you've sold that pig, watch out for beggars and cutpurses," she warned.

"The market's full of 'em."

Arthur felt his throat tighten. He didn't want to sell his pig one little bit. Henry had been the runt of a litter and Arthur had brought him up on his own. Now Henry was more like a dog than a pig. He could sit, fetch and do all sorts of tricks.

He even came to a reed whistle
Arthur had made. Well,
sometimes he did. But
now Henry was huge
and always hungry, and there just weren't
enough scraps to feed him.

"Jack Jones says the King's hunting in
the forest today," said Arthur, stuffing the
last of last week's bread in his pocket. It
would do for his lunch. "Jack says he often
comes to the tavern for a drop of ale."
Arthur tried to imagine what King Henry
might look like. He probably wore a
doublet of silk embroidered with gold and
a fine velvet hat stuck with jewels and
feathers. "I might even see him," he said
dreamily.

"All the more reason to look your best,"
replied his mother. "Better'n Jack Jones

anyway," she muttered under her breath.
"And you stay away from that tavern,"
she added sternly. "As for them Joneses—"

"I'll be off then," interrupted Arthur,
jumping up from the table. He knew his
mother was about to tell him for the
hundredth time about her feud with Mrs
Jones next door. His father and Mr Jones
had run off to sea. Mrs Jones had blamed
Old Mother Knucklebone. "You and your
potions," she had screamed. "You put a
spell on 'em! You're a witch, you are!"

"Superstitious old crone," muttered Mrs Knucklebone as she hauled a pile of dripping bedclothes out of a wooden tub, "believe *anything*, she could."

Mind you, thought Old Mother Knucklebone as she dragged the bedclothes towards the door, in my line of business those sort of people make the best patients.

Outside in the garden Arthur blew Henry's whistle. A minute

later a huge spotted pig thundered out of
the hedgerow with half a cabbage clamped
in his jaws.

"Oh no," whispered Arthur and he ran
as fast as he could across the meadow, his
mother's shouts ringing in his ears and
Henry galloping behind him.

2
A Penny For Henry

Halfway across a field, Arthur suddenly realised Henry was no longer with him. He had been daydreaming about running away to sea like his father and had forgotten all about his pig.

Arthur turned round and spied the

blurred outline of something big and spotted.

It was Henry. Henry could never resist acorns.

Arthur blew his whistle and shouted. He clapped his hands and shouted louder. But nothing happened. Henry wasn't moving for anyone.

Stupid, stubborn pig! muttered Arthur to

himself. You're more trouble than you're
worth. Serve you right to go to market!

It took Arthur ages to reach the oak tree
and by the time he got there he was in a
filthy temper. Henry, on the other hand,
was full of acorns and lying happily in a
shallow bed of cool fresh earth.

"Henry!" yelled Arthur, prodding him
with his foot. "Get up!"

Henry looked up with his clever piggy eyes and slowly got to his feet. It was then that Arthur noticed something, half buried, glinting in the sunshine. It was a penny. Henry must have dug it up as he rooted about for acorns.

Arthur's heart leapt to his throat. A penny was a fortune to him. Now there were all sorts of things he could do at the market. He could go and see the jugglers and the acrobats. Or he could gamble at the cock-fight. He could even buy himself a new bow and arrow. Old Mother Knucklebone liked birds, especially song birds. The sweeter the tune, the sweeter the taste, she always said.

Arthur picked up the penny. Henry was watching him. It was almost as if he was reading his mind. Suddenly Arthur felt flushed and guilty.

He stared at the penny. He knew that if he kept it and took it back to his mother, he wouldn't have to sell Henry after all.

"What are you doing standing there like a daft donkey?" shouted a voice behind him.

Arthur closed his hand over the penny.

It was Jack Jones from next door. He was herding a gaggle of geese in front of him and by the swarm of bees that followed the wicker basket on his back Arthur knew he was carrying honeycombs to market.

"You coming shin-kicking?" asked Jack. "All the lads'll be there." He grinned and kicked Arthur in the shins. "Lasses too.

A lass likes a clever lad, I'm told."

Arthur looked at Jack's sturdy new boots and then at his own ragged shoes. He didn't like shin-kicking at the best of times. And he wasn't due another pair of shoes this year. But he wasn't going to tell that to Jack.

"Not me," he said grandly. "I fancy a gamble at the cock-fight."

"Oh yeah," sneered Jack. "Since when are the Knucklebones richer than the Joneses?"

At that moment a pretty girl with her hair coiled above her head walked past them. She was pushing a barrow of cheeses and leading a goat with two kids.

Jack and Arthur stared after her.

"That's Molly Mayflower," said Jack in a low voice. "Not married yet neither."

"How do you know?" whispered Arthur.

"She ain't wearing a hat, stupid," said Jack. "Maids go bareheaded, maids do."

"Coming to market, lads?" called Molly Mayflower in a high tinkling voice. It was just how Arthur imagined a silver bell would sound.

He stared at Molly's heart-shaped face and her smiling red mouth. Arthur thought she was the loveliest girl he had ever seen.

Thwack! Jack kicked him in the shins again.

Molly blushed and hid her smile behind her hands.

"Didn't I tell you a lass likes a good shin-kicker," said Jack knowingly.

"That so?" said Arthur, rubbing his shin. But he wasn't going to kick back. In fact he was sorry for Jack. He felt the penny in his hand. Molly would also like a lad who bought her a present of fine lace.

In his mind's eye, Arthur saw Molly staring into his face with her beautiful blue eyes, smiling only at him. Then he looked down. Henry was watching him. Once again Arthur felt flushed and guilty.

A penny's worth of lace would be a poor trade for a pig like Henry.

3
Mad Michael's Revenge

Jack and Arthur could hear the market
well before they reached the village square.
Sheep bleated, cows mooed. Wooden
cartwheels creaked and rattled as they
wobbled over the pitted road. And over the
top of everything were voices. *Finest pears!*

Buy my fish! Best flour for your bread!

An enormous crowd of people jostled and pushed in front of them. There were women with huge baskets of freshly baked loaves and men leading ponies, their saddlebags stuffed with carrots and turnips and long strings of onions. There were boys carrying poles hung about with flapping chickens and small girls holding up aprons full of hazelnuts, posies of marigolds clutched in their hands.

On one side of the square, painted signs hung outside shops that leaned this way and that over the dirt road. Arthur saw three silver fishes for the fishmonger.

He would buy his six herrings there. The next sign was a pair of scissors. Scissors for cutting cloth, thought Arthur, feeling pleased with himself.

That's where he could buy the brown woollen cloth. He saw three brushes for the broom maker and a golden key for the locksmith and a bridle and stirrups told him where the saddler lived. Not that Arthur could ever imagine owning a horse.

Suddenly a roaring and yelping drowned the noise of the crowd. "Look!" cried Jack, yanking Arthur's sleeve. "There's a *bear* dancing on the green!"

"It's not dancing," said Arthur, pulling his arm away. For once he knew something that Jack didn't. "Those dogs are biting it. It's called bear-baiting."

Beside them a flat-topped cart rumbled to a stop. A man dressed in a blue coat trimmed with rabbit fur was standing on top of it. *"Come hear our story!"* he cried. *"A tale of fame and fortune! A tale of dreams come true. A young man yearns for London! That young man could be you!"*

Arthur stared back at the bright eyes in the grinning face. A strange feeling prickled the back of his neck. Could this man be reading his thoughts? Because sometimes

Arthur *did* dream of running away to London. Sometimes, during the long dark evenings when rain soaked through the thatch roof and the smell of the iron pot grew almost too horrible to bear, he yearned to live in a palace and wear fine clothes like people in London did.

"Huh," said Jack. "I ain't listening to no fairy stories." He pulled a face. "London. Might as well be the moon for the likes of us." Then his voice changed. "Arthur," he said slowly. He sounded almost frightened.

"Why is that man staring at you?"

"What man?" said
Arthur.

Jack pointed to the
tavern. Sitting
outside it was a huge
man with bulging
eyes and a wild black

beard. His skin was as lumpy and grey as
the boulder he was leaning against.

Arthur's stomach went cold. "That's
Mad Michael," he said in a hoarse
whisper. As he spoke he could feel his
knees knocking. Mad Michael was the
blacksmith and the most ferocious man in
the village. What's more he had sworn
revenge on all Knucklebones ever since
Old Mother Knucklebone had sold him an
ointment for belly ache.

Arthur shuddered. It was one of his
mother's prize ointments. She ground up
chicken necks, crushed worms and fox fat
and mixed the whole lot with mole's blood.

And not just any mole's blood. Arthur had to catch one under a full moon on a rainy night.

The trouble was that Mad Michael had got the instructions wrong and instead of rubbing a little of the ointment on his belly each day at noon, he had eaten the whole lot on the first day at midnight.

And Mad Michael had never been the same since.

Arthur watched in horror as the big man banged down his tankard of Dragon's Milk, stood up and fixed him with bloodshot eyes.

There was no time to lose.

"See you later," yelled Arthur. And, to Jack's amazement, he turned and ran down the nearest alley.

He didn't see the pedlar standing

halfway down with his tray of silks and ribbons and fancy lace.

Which is why Arthur ran slap bang into him, knocking the tray and everything in it to the ground.

4

Arthur In Trouble Again

"You clumsy bullock!" yelled the pedlar.
His face was white with fury. "Why can't
you look where you're going?" Around
them the ground was suddenly a carpet of
reds, blues and yellows. Ribbons uncoiled
like glittering snakes, silks sparkled in the

sun and lacy handkerchiefs lay like snowflakes on the dusty road.

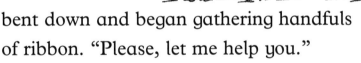

Arthur stood for a moment staring dumbly at his feet. "I beg your pardon," he mumbled. He bent down and began gathering handfuls of ribbon. "Please, let me help you."

"Orright, orright," muttered the pedlar, shaking out silks and arranging them on his tray. "Just mind that bit of lace in front of you. It's a penny's worth of my finest and I can't sell it dirty."

Arthur picked up the lace and held it in his fingers. It was light as a feather and delicately worked in a pattern of flowers.

Flowers, he thought. Just like her name, Mayflower. Molly Mayflower.

He reached for the penny in his purse.

"Oi!" roared an angry voice. "Get that pig out of here!"

Arthur jumped up. Henry was staring hungrily at a bunch of carrots hanging over the side of a vegetable seller's stall.

"Henry!" yelled Arthur. He dropped the piece of lace and ran towards the stall as his enormous pig edged closer and closer to the carrots. "Henry!" he yelled again.

But he was too late. The bunch of carrots disappeared down Henry's throat and he was already heading towards a pile of tasty-looking cabbages.

"I said get that pig out of

here!" yelled the vegetable man, grabbing a stout stick and waving it.

But Henry wasn't afraid. He knew how to dodge sticks. He grabbed a cabbage and scrambled underneath the stall.

"Henry!" shouted Arthur desperately. "Come here!"

"Who's Henry?" roared the vegetable man. He had a face like a spotty potato and a nose the colour of beetroot.

"Henry's a pig!" explained Arthur panting so much he could hardly speak.

"HENRY'S A PIG!" roared the vegetable man. His weed-coloured eyes rolled in his face. "HENRY'S A PIG?"

"Arrest him! Arrest him!" bellowed a harsh voice. "He's insulted the King!"

Arthur spun round and found himself staring up into the bulging, bloodshot eyes of Mad Michael.

"I have *not* insulted the King!" cried
Arthur, his heart hammering in his chest.
"Henry's a pig. He's *my* p —" He couldn't
say any more because Mad Michael
clamped a filthy hand over his mouth.

Out of the
corner of his
eye, Arthur
saw Henry
squeeze out
from under
the stall and
thunder
away, another bunch of carrots hanging
from his mouth.

Then everything went black and Arthur
was in the middle of a howling crowd
being dragged over the dusty ground.

All around him, men and women were yelling: "Whip him! Brand him! Cut off his ears! Chop off his hands!"

Then somebody shouted, "Hang him!"

Arthur closed his eyes. He saw the hanging tree. He saw the noose. He saw his life pass in front of him. And it wasn't much of a life, he thought miserably.

"Silence!" roared a voice. It was a voice louder and more frightening than any Arthur had ever heard before.

He opened his eyes. At first he thought

he was dreaming. So he closed them.
Then he opened them again.

He wasn't dreaming.

In front of him was a big red-headed
man on a huge white horse. The man held
a tankard of ale in his hand. His doublet
was made of the finest leather worked with
precious stones. A gold
medallion hung
round his neck.

Arthur
Knucklebone
opened his
eyes wide and
stared into
the face of
Henry VIII,
King of
England.

5

A Dream Come True

"What on earth is going on here?"
bellowed King Henry, his sharp eyes
blazing with anger. "I come to your village
for rest and refreshment and what do I
find?" He paused. "PANDEMONIUM!"

The words echoed round the square.

The crowd went silent. You could almost hear the knees knocking, thought Arthur afterwards.

"Well?" demanded the King. "Are you dumb as well as unruly?"

Still nobody spoke.

"Begging your humble pardon, Your Humbleness," croaked Mad Michael, half crawling, half walking forward. "This man here insulted your Royal Excellence."

"What man?" shouted the King.

Mad Michael held up Arthur like a wet chicken.

King Henry stared at Arthur. "That's no man," he said. "That's a mere lad."

"He said a *terrible* thing, Sire," insisted

Mad Michael in a whining whisper. "He called you a pig."

A mutter rippled through the crowd. "Cut off his ears. Chop off his hands. Rip out his tongue, I would."

Arthur moaned. If only he had chosen another name for his pig. If only he had followed his mother's advice. "There's no point pretending, son," she had said. "Call him Porkchops and be done with it."

Arthur moaned again.

"Bring the boy forward!" commanded the King. Arthur could hardly believe his ears. He shook himself free from Mad Michael and knelt before his King. The strange thing was that he couldn't help noting how King Henry's eyes looked just like Henry's. They were piggy and cunning and they seemed to be reading his mind.

"Speak," commanded the King.

"I, er, called my pig Henry," stuttered Arthur. He was so frightened, it was almost impossible to speak. "Because he was so beautiful and so clever learning his tricks." Arthur took a trembling breath. "So when I called 'Henry!', I was calling my pig." He stared at his ragged shoes. "I would *never* insult you, Sire, never!"

The King motioned for another tankard of ale. "And this pig called Henry," he said in a dangerous voice, "Where is he?"

"He ran off with a bunch of carrots, Sire," said Arthur.

"So," replied the King, "how do I know you are telling me the truth?"

Arthur felt for the reed whistle in his pocket. "I'll call him, Your Wonderfulness," he said quickly. "It's one of his tricks. He comes to a whistle."

"Does he now?" said the King. "That *is* clever." He stared at Arthur. "Call him."

With trembling fingers, Arthur put the whistle to his mouth and blew.

No Henry.

Arthur blew the whistle again. Harder this time.

No Henry.

The crowd began muttering. King Henry's face darkened. He leaned forward. "If you're lying to me, boy..." he said.

Now Arthur was shaking so hard, he could hardly stand up. Where was Henry?

Suddenly Arthur remembered the one sound that Henry could never resist. "May I have a bucket?" he croaked.

The crowd roared with laughter.

King Henry held up his hand for silence. "Bring the lad a bucket!" he ordered.

Arthur knew this was his last chance. He put the whistle to his mouth and, just like he did every morning when he gave Henry his breakfast scraps, he blew it as hard as he could and rattled the bucket.

A low rumble was heard from the end of an alley. There was a thunder of hooves and, within seconds, a huge spotted pig burst into the square, an enormous turnip held fast in his jaws.

It was Henry!

"Give!" commanded Arthur.

Henry dropped the turnip at Arthur's feet. Arthur picked it up and threw it onto the other side of the square. "Fetch!" he said.

Henry galloped across the square, picked up the turnip and brought it back.

"Good pig," said Arthur, taking the turnip from his mouth. "Roll over then *sit*!"

Which is exactly what Henry did.

The crowd gasped.

King Henry held out his hand for *another* tankard of ale.

He looked at Arthur. He looked at the huge spotted pig chomping happily on his turnip. Then he threw back his head and laughed until tears ran down his face.

"That pig is smarter than almost every minister in my palace," cried the King. He turned to the group of courtiers behind him. "What say you? Shall I make him Ambassador to France?"

The courtiers looked sideways at each other and tittered nervously.

"What is your name, boy?" cried the King.

"Arthur Knucklebone, Sire," said Arthur, bowing as best he could.

The King reached into his pocket and pulled out two gold sovereigns. "I should like to buy your pig," he said. "He is the cleverest pig I have ever seen. It is an honour to share his name." And with that King Henry slapped the two gold coins into Arthur's hand.

56

Arthur was dumbfounded. Two gold sovereigns was more than a craftsman earned in a year.

Suddenly the crowd parted and Old Mother Knucklebone strode into the square. She didn't seem to notice the big pink-faced man on a horse.

"You sold that pig yet?" she cried. "I 'eard there was going to be an 'anging so I came to market after all."

Arthur opened his mouth to speak when Jack Jones and Molly Mayflower came arm in arm around the corner. Jack looked so pleased with himself that he didn't notice the big man either.

"You missed the shin-kicking," sneered Jack. He smirked at Molly. "What did I tell ya? I *knows* what a lass likes."

Arthur stared at his mother's beaky
face. He stared at Jack's black and blue
shins and Molly Mayflower hanging on his
arm. He'd had enough of the smelly

potions and the straw bed above the
stables. He'd had enough of the feud with
the Joneses next door. And as for Molly,

Arthur decided he had never really liked her in the first place.

He felt the sovereigns in his pocket and thought of the words of the actor's song. *A tale of fame and fortune. A tale of dreams come true. A young man yearns for London. That young man could be you!*

At that moment Arthur Knucklebone made the biggest decision of his life. He reached into his purse and handed his mother back her penny. Then he gave her one of his sovereigns.

"Goodbye," he said, kissing her leathery cheek. "I'll see you in London."

Before his mother could

reply, the huge pink-faced man signalled for his courtiers. Suddenly Old Mother Knucklebone realised who the big man was. But it was as if she was under some kind of spell.

Old Mother Knucklebone stood frozen like a statue and, even though her mouth went up and down, no sound came out.

Henry VIII put his jewelled hand on Arthur's shoulder. "Pig Trainer to the Royal Household," said King Henry in a low voice. "Are you with me, lad?"

Arthur Knucklebone's heart exploded. His head spun. And the smile that appeared on his face stretched from ear to ear. "I'm with you, Sire," he cried.

Tudor country life

In this story Arthur Knucklebone is a made-up character, but his life as a Tudor country boy was very real.

Tudor schools

Arthur Knucklebone did not like school (pages 12-13). He went to a 'Dame' school in his village where he was taught the alphabet and simple sums. There were no books though. Classes began very early and ended late. Children were beaten or whipped if they didn't remember what they were taught. No wonder Arthur didn't like his school.

Tudor houses

Tudor houses for ordinary people were pretty grim too. Arthur's house was a run-down cottage (pages 6-7). We would call it a hovel. It was dark, damp and smelly. There was a fire in one corner and a hole in the roof for smoke to escape. The floor was just beaten earth.

Tudor food

The food for poor people like the Knucklebones was terrible. They ate mostly bread and vegetables, and perhaps a rabbit or hare now and again—if they managed to catch one.

Tudor medicines

Tudor medicines were very like Mrs Knucklebone's potions (pages 8-10). And if these didn't make you better (and they usually made you worse) a cut was made in a vein to let the 'bad blood' run out. This was called blood-letting and was a cure for most illnesses. If you were seriously ill in Tudor times, you usually died.

Tudor fairs

But Tudor life wasn't all bad. Village fairs and markets were

fun for everyone. Farmers' wives would take their produce, such as chickens, hams and eggs, to sell. Pedlars travelled from village to village with trays of lace, ribbons, toys and needles. It was a tray like this that Arthur knocked over.

Tudor fun

There were many entertainments, although they were often very cruel. Bear-baiting (page 33), cock-fighting, even watching some poor

beggar being hanged were all thought to be fun things to do. Boys played rough sports. Jack Jones was keen on shin-kicking. Cudgelling was another favourite. Two players had a club each and then tried to hit each other over the head. The winner was the one still standing at the end of the game.

Life in the country was hard for Arthur. Can you blame him for running off to London?